D0934636

– in –

Trendsetter

visit us at
www.abdopublishing.com

Exclusive Spotlight library bound edition published in 2007 by Spotlight, a division of ABDO Publishing Group, Edina, Minnesota. Spotlight produces high quality reinforced library bound editions for schools and libraries. Published by agreement with Archie Comic Publications, Inc.

Library of Congress Cataloging-in-Publication Data

Betty and Veronica in Trendsetter / edited by Nelson Ribeiro & Victor Gorelick.
p. cm. -- (The Archie digest library)
Revision of issue no. 118 (March 2001) of Betty and Veronica digest magazine.
ISBN-13: 978-1-59961-268-3
ISBN-10: 1-59961-268-2
I. Ribeiro, Nelson. II. Gorelick, Victor. III. Betty and Veronica digest magazine. 118. IV. Title: Trendsetter.

PN6728.A72B53 2007
741.5'973--dc22

2006050552

All Spotlight books are reinforced library binding
and manufactured in the United States of America.

Contents

Betty and Veronica

LOOK! MOLLY'S CREW IS TRYING TO SET ANOTHER FASHION TREND!
...THE NOUVEAU BOHEMIAN LOOK!
Betty & Veronica in "Trend Setter"

SCRIPT: GEORGE GLADIR PENCILS: TIM KENNEDY INKS: KEN SELIG
COLORS: FRANK GAGLIARDO LETTERS: BILL YOSHIDA
EDITORS: NELSON RIBEIRO & VICTOR GORELICK EDITOR-IN-CHIEF: RICHARD GOLDWATER

LET'S SHOW THOSE FASHION MAVENS HOW TO REALLY SET A TREND!
FWIP! FWIP!

WHERE ARE YOU OFF TO, VERONICA?
YOU'LL SEE?

I'D LIKE TO SEE SOME TRENDY SANDALS!
WE ALWAYS KEEP SOME IN STOCK ... EVEN THOUGH IT'S WINTER!
Le Shoe Store

SANDALS IN WINTER?
WHY NOT?

SO WHICH DO YOU PREFER?
IT'S GONNA BE HARD TO CHOOSE!
NO... IT WON'T, NANCY...

I'LL TAKE 'EM ALL!
ALL?!

THE FOLLOWING MONDAY...
HA! HA! VERONICA'S DOING SANDALS!

ANYTHING TO BE DIFFERENT!
BUT OF COURSE!
... SINCE I AM DIFFERENT!
2

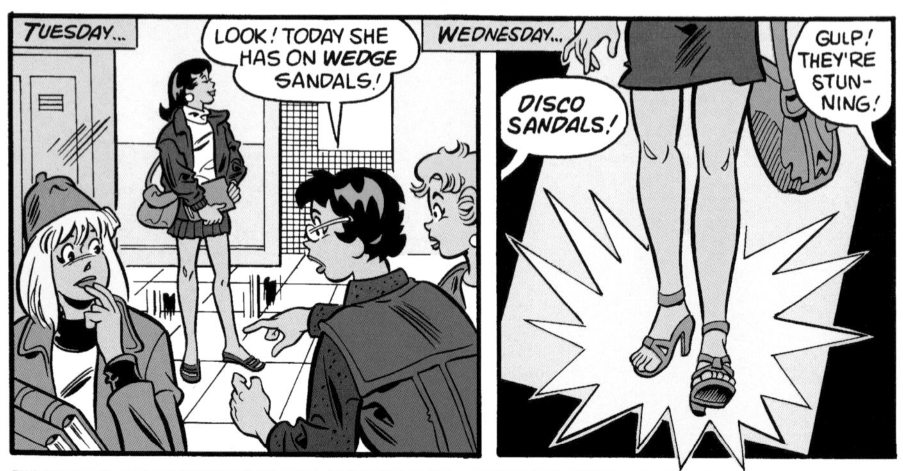
TUESDAY...
LOOK! TODAY SHE HAS ON WEDGE SANDALS!
WEDNESDAY...
DISCO SANDALS!
GULP! THEY'RE STUN-NING!

YOU'RE REALLY GETTING TO MOLLY'S GANG WITH THIS SANDALS THING!
TOMORROW WE'LL REALLY DO THEM IN!

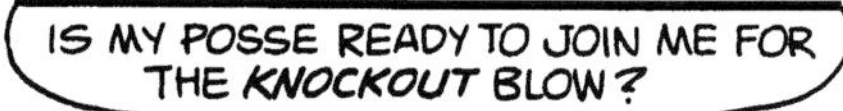
IS MY POSSE READY TO JOIN ME FOR THE KNOCKOUT BLOW?

THURSDAY...
HMPF! NOW ALL OF VERONICA'S FRIENDS ARE INTO IT!
GULP! THAT TOENAIL POLISH DOES LOOK KINDA COOL!
3

FRIDAY...
I JUST ADORE YOUR TOE KNOB SANDALS!
MOLLY GRIFFITH'S GANG HAS JUST CAVED IN!
THEY'RE FOLLOW-ING OUR TREND!

LOOKS LIKE ALMOST THE WHOLE SCHOOL IS INTO SANDALS!

ACTUALLY, I'D SAY EVERYONE IS INTO IT!

CHECK OUT, MISS GRUNDY!
4

THE WEEKEND ROLLS AROUND...
MONDAY, WE'RE GOING TO DRIVE MOLLY'S GANG INTO A TIZZY!
POP'S
COLD FRONT HEADED THIS WAY

WE'RE STARTING A NEW SHOE FAD!
PLATFORM BOOTS!
OOOHH!

MONDAY...
HA! JUST LOOK AT WHAT THOSE DITZES ARE INTO NOW!

IF YOU THINK YOU'RE STAMPEDING US INTO ANOTHER SCREWBALL TREND, YOU'VE GOT ANOTHER THINK COMING!
TOO BAD!

AREN'T THOSE SNOW FLURRIES I DETECT?
5

BRRR... MY TOOTSIES ARE FREEZING!
AND OURS ARE WARM AND TOASTY!
SO ARE MINE!!
TUESDAY...
LOOKS LIKE YOUR GANG HAS EVERY-ONE INTO PLATFORMS!
YES, WE BELIEVE IN TAKING FASHION TO A HIGHER LEVEL!
ONLY NOW, ALL YOU GIRLS ARE TALLER THAN US GUYS!
BUT THAT'S AS IT SHOULD BE, ARCHIE...
WE BELIEVE BOYS SHOULD ALWAYS LOOK UP TO GIRLS!
END

Betty and Veronica
-in-
"SELF DEFENSED"
SEE YOU LATER, DADDYKINS! BETTY AND I ARE GOING OUT!
NEWS
MORGAN'S DEPT. STORE
MUGGINGS ROBBERY
CRIME UP

BE CAREFUL AND KEEP AN EYE OUT FOR TROUBLE!
OH, DON'T WORRY! BETTY HAS BEEN TAKING KARATE CLASSES!

THAT'S RIGHT, MR. LODGE! I BELIEVE EVERYONE NEEDS A DEFENSE MECHA-NISM! MINE IS KARATE...HEE-YAH!

YOU KNOW, BETTY, VERONICA SHOULD LEARN PERSONAL DEFENSE, TOO!
HUMPH! I'D RATHER HAVE A LINE OF PERSONAL CREDIT!

WELL, I THINK SIGNING YOU UP FOR SOME SELF DEFENSE CLASSES IS A GOOD IDEA!

LATER AT BETTY'S KARATE SCHOOL...
I DON'T LIKE THIS, DADDYKINS!
WHY NOT?
HEE-YAH!

EVERYONE HERE WEARS THE SAME DRAB OUTFIT!

MS. CHOE, THESE ARE THE LODGES!
WELCOME!
2

I'D LIKE MY DAUGHTER TO LEARN SOME FORM OF SELF DEFENSE!
THAT IS OUR SPECIALTY!

WE WILL FIND WHICH OF THE MARTIAL ARTS IS BEST SUITED TO YOUR DAUGHTER ... KARATE ... JUDO ... KUNG FU ... ETC.

BEFORE WE START, I HAVE ONE IMPORTANT QUESTION!
YES?

CAN I AT LEAST ACCESSORIZE MY OUTFIT?
?
!
?

A WEEK LATER...
HOW'S RON DOING, MS. CHOE?
NOT TOO WELL, BETTY! SHE MAY NOT BE SUITED FOR THIS TYPE OF DEFENSE!
3

TRY THIS FLYING KICK, RON! HEE-YAH!
HUMPH! NO WAY!!

WHY NOT? TOO HARD? TOO HIGH? TOO DIFFICULT?
NO! NO! NO!

IT'LL MESS UP MY HAIR!
I SEE WHAT YOU MEAN, MS. CHOE!

I HOPE WE CAN FIND A SUITABLE PERSONAL DEFENSE FOR HER BY THE TIME WE HAVE OUR MONTHLY OPEN HOUSE!
ME, TOO! HER DAD IS CONCERNED ABOUT HER SAFETY!

AT THE OPEN HOUSE...
SO WHAT IS RON'S BEST DEFENSIVE MANEUVER, MS. CHOE?
HMMM... FOR NOW, SHE'LL ATTEMPT A JUDO THROW!
4

HEE-YUK!
OOF!
OH NO!
SNAP
NO! NO! YES!
I BROKE MY LONGEST NAIL!
GASP!
EEEEEK!
YIPES! LET ME OUT OF HERE!

MR. LODGE, WE FINALLY FOUND RON'S BEST DEFENSE MECHANISM... HER VOICE!
WOW! WHAT STRONG LUNGS!

A SCREAM LIKE THAT WOULD FRIGHTEN AWAY MOST ATTACKERS AND BRING HELP FAST!
AND I DON'T EVEN NEED VOICE TRAINING!
The End

LIFE CAN BE VERY UNPREDICTABLE AT TIMES!
A HAPPY MOMENT CAN SUDDENLY TURN INTO A BIG, BIG DISAPPOINTMENT!
...SOME EXAMPLES...
Betty in "A TWIST OF FATE"

I WAS ECSTATIC WHEN MY PHONE RANG! I WAS EXPECTING A CALL FROM A NEW BOY IN CLASS...
...BUT I COULDN'T FIND MY PHONE IN THE MESS!
IN CONCERT
IT'S HIM! IT'S HIM!
BETTY
RRINNNNNGG!!
DARN! WHERE IS IT? ...WHERE IS IT?
RINNNGGG!
RINNNGGG!
RINNNGG!
BY THE TIME I DID FIND IT, MY HANDSOME HUNK HAD HUNG UP!

ANOTHER EXAMPLE OF LIFE'S UNPREDICTABILITY...
I HAD SPENT ALL DAY SEARCHING FOR A DRESS TO WEAR TO THE JUNIOR PROM...
DRESSING ROOM

I MUST HAVE TRIED ON HUNDREDS OF OUTFITS!
NO WAY!

FINALLY, I FOUND THE DREAM NUMBER! RIGHT SIZE... RIGHT COLOR... RIGHT PRICE!

AS I EXITED THE MALL, I WAS IN A STATE OF BLISS...
IT'S PERFECT IN EVERY WAY!

LATER, I WAS DEVASTATED WHEN I SPOTTED THREE OTHERS WEARING THE IDENTICAL "PERFECT DRESS"!

AND THEN THERE WAS THE TIME PROF. FLUTESNOOT DECIDED TO PAIR OFF EVERYONE WITH A LAB PARTNER...

I WAS HOPING AGAINST HOPE MY PARTNER WOULD BE... A CERTAIN "SOMEONE"...
VERONICA WILL TEAM UP WITH... DILTON!

WHEN IT WAS MY TURN, THE SUSPENSE WAS UNBEARABLE...
BETTY WILL PAIR WITH...
...ARCHIE!

I WAS ECSTATIC! I HAD GOTTEN MY DREAM LAB PARTNER!

...UNFORTUNATELY!
SORRY ABOUT THAT!
3

AND HOW CAN I FORGET THE TIME ARCHIE INVITED ME TO WATCH A VIDEO ?...

I WAS ALL SET TO SPEND A COZY AND ROMANTIC EVENING...

...ONLY TO FIND OUT ARCHIE HAD CHOSEN A GRADE B HORROR MOVIE!
I ALSO HAVE THE SEQUELS TO "WORM"! ..."WORM II"... AND "WORM III"!
VHS
WORM II

OF COURSE, SOMETIMES THE REVERSE CAN OCCUR...

...LIKE THE DAY I WOKE UP TO DISCOVER IT WAS FRIDAY THE THIRTEENTH...
FEB
13
FRIDAY

...AND MY HOROSCOPE PREDICTED ALL SORTS OF DIRE CONSEQUENCES!
FAILURE
MISFORTUNE
DISASTER
RIVERDALE HERALD
4

I FEARED THE WORST AS I ENTERED SCHOOL...
(GULP!) - A BLACK CAT CROSSING MY PATH!
RIVERDALE HIGH SCHOOL

...ONLY TO BE GREETED BY THE NEWS THAT I HAD MADE THE HONOR ROLL...
WITH A STRAIGHT "A" AVERAGE!

...AND THAT I HAD ALSO BEEN CHOSEN HOMECOMING QUEEN!!

AND LATER THAT SAME DAY, MY MISSING CAT TURNED UP SAFE AND SOUND!

LIKE I SAID, "LIFE CAN BE VERY UNPREDICTABLE AT TIMES!"
End

ARCHIE, YOU'LL HAVE TO BE VERY QUIET! DADDY IS STILL SLEEPING!
HE WAS UP ALL NIGHT WORKING ON AN ARTICLE A PRESTIGIOUS MAGAZINE ASKED HIM TO WRITE!
OKAY! I'LL BE AS QUIET AS A MOUSE!
Veronica IN "BACKUPS"
CRASH!
OOOOPS!
YOU MEAN A MOOSE!
ARCHIE, IS THAT YOU?
BANG
CLANK
CLATTER
1

I'M SORRY, MR. LODGE! I DIDN'T MEAN TO WAKE YOU!
THAT'S ALL RIGHT, MY BOY!

I'VE HAD A REFRESHING NAP, AND TODAY I SUBMIT AN ARTICLE THAT I WROTE WHICH I'M QUITE PROUD OF!

IT TOOK ME HOURS OF SHAPING IT AND ADDING AND DELETING WORDS AND PHRASES TO GET IT JUST PERFECT!

THESE WORD PROCESSORS ARE MARVELOUS DEVICES! I'VE GOT THE WHOLE TEXT RIGHT IN HERE!
R

WOULD YOU LIKE TO SEE IT?
SURE, MR. LODGE!
ARCHIE, NO! DON'T TOUCH IT!
R

NONSENSE, VERONICA! I'M SURE THE BOY KNOWS HOW TO OPERATE ONE OF THESE!
SURE! WE LEARNED IT IN SCHOOL!
2

THERE'S THE TEXT! DO YOU KNOW HOW TO ADVANCE IT?
SURE! YOU JUST PRESS THIS KEY...

OR IS IT THIS ONE OR... UH-OH!
ARCHIE, YOU'VE ERASED IT!

RUN, ARCHIE! I'LL TRY TO CALM DADDY DOWN!

THAT WON'T BE NECESSARY! THERE'S NO PROBLEM!
DADDY, THE VEINS IN YOUR NECK AREN'T STANDING OUT!

THAT'S RIGHT! YOU SEE, REALIZING THAT THERE COULD BE AN UNFORE-SEEN CALAMITY SUCH AS ARCHIE, I TOOK PRECAUTIONS!

I MADE THIS BACKUP DISC AND I'LL USE IT TO REFORMAT THE ONE THAT WAS ERASED!
3

NOW, HOW DO YOU DO THIS, AGAIN?
I THINK YOU HAVE TO PRESS THIS KEY, OR IS IT THIS ONE?

OH, NO! ARCHIE, YOU DID IT AGAIN! YOU'VE ERASED THE BACKUP DISC!

QUICK, MAKE A BREAK FOR IT, BEFORE IT ALL SINKS IN!
TUT, TUT, TUT, TUT, TUT TUT!

FIGURING THAT EVEN THE BACK-UP DISC COULD BE ERASED, I TOOK FURTHER PRECAUTIONS...

I MADE A HARD COPY!
BOY! THAT'S SURE LUCKY!

OOOPS!
ARCHIE, NO! NOW YOU'VE REALLY DONE IT!
4

IT'S ALL MESSED UP!
FORTUNATELY, FIGURING THAT SOMETHING LIKE THAT COULD HAPPEN, I MADE A PHOTOCOPY...

AND YOU'RE NOT GETTING YOUR HANDS ON THIS!

THIS IS THE LAST COPY OF THE TEXT LEFT, AND I'M NOT TAKING ANY CHANCES ON YOU TRASHING IT, SO STAY BACK!

I'M GOING TO RUN OFF A HUNDRED MORE COPIES OF IT BEFORE ANYTHING ELSE HAPPENS!

NO, DADDY, DON'T! THAT'S NOT THE PHOTOCOPY MACHINE...

IT'S THE PAPER SHREDDER!
I THINK NOW IS THE TIME TO MAKE A BREAK FOR IT!
END

I'M GLAD YOU WORK HERE, ETHEL!
YOU CAN HELP ME CHOOSE A PET!
RABBITS ARE CUTE, BUT THEY MULTIPLY SO RAPIDLY!
Betty IN "PET SET"
AND TROPICAL FISH ARE BEAUTIFUL! BUT THEY REQUIRE SO MUCH CARE...
WELL, BETTY, ...BETTY?!! WHERE DID THE GIRL DISAPPEAR TO?
I THINK SHE JUST FOUND THE PET SHE WAS LOOKING FOR!
END

Betty in "COVER STORY"

ER... DO I HEAR SQUEALS OF ENTHUSIASM, DEAR?
LOOK, DADDY! ISN'T HE SIMPLY SCRUMPTIOUS!
FILM-PIX
BRAD

I DO BELIEVE OUR GIRL HAS FOUND A NEW LOVE, DEAR!
NONSENSE! NO ONE WILL EVER REPLACE ARCHIE!

YOU SHOULD HEAR HER GUSH OVER THIS MONTH'S "FILM PIX"!
I GUSHED A LOT WHEN I WAS HER AGE, TOO!

HMMM... REMEMBER THAT PICTURE WE THREW OUT LAST WEEK?
THE ONE THAT FADED SO BADLY FROM THE SUN! WHAT ABOUT IT?

WELL, THE FRAME WAS STILL USABLE, SO I SAVED IT!
SO?
?

GOTTA RETURN A LIBRARY BOOK, MOM! I'LL BE BACK SOON!
ALL RIGHT, DEAR!
2

EEEP! I'M BEGINNING TO FEEL FLUSHED!-AND I KNOW EXACTLY WHAT IT IS!
RIVERDALE LIBRARY

IT'S THE FLUSH OF GUILT!! WHAT WOULD ARCHIE SAY IF HE KNEW HOW SILLY I GOT OVER THAT MAGAZINE COVER?
NON FICTION
RETURN BOOKS HERE

SURE, BRAD FREEMAN IS GORGEOUS, ALL RIGHT, BUT ARCHIE IS... WELL... ARCHIE!-AND HE'S REAL! (SIGH!)
LIBRARY
TRIP!

DEAR, YOU DIDN'T LOOK THAT SAD WHEN YOU LEFT FOR THE LIBRARY!
DON'T WORRY! YOUR OL' DAD DID SOMETHING THAT'LL CHEER YOU UP!

WHAT IS IT, DADDY?
UP IN YOUR ROOM... IT'S A SURPRISE!

WELL, A NICE SURPRISE MIGHT TAKE MY MIND OFF MY GUILTY CONSCIENCE...
3

HMMM? I DON'T SEE ANY SURPRISE!
... I WONDER WHAT DADDY WAS...

SCREEECH!!

AAARGH! H-HE FRAMED BRAD FREEMAN!-AND IT'S A NICER FRAME THAN ARCHIE'S!
BRAD

LISTEN TO THOSE SCREAMS OF JOY! I GUESS GOOD OL' DAD DID THE RIGHT THING!
I'M NOT TOO SURE THAT'S JOY!

WHAT FATHER... I SAY, WHAT FATHER WOULD DO A TERRIBLE THING LIKE THIS TO HIS OWN DAUGHTER?!
HUH?!!

ARE YOU TRYING TO DESTROY ME? OH, HOW COULD YOU?
NICE WORK, DEAR OL' DAD!
SNIFF! SOB!
4

WHAT WOULD ARCHIE THINK, IF HE COULD SEE THIS SILLY PICTURE NEXT TO HIS ON MY DRESSER?!

OUT! OUT! I'LL BE GUILT-RIDDEN FOR A WEEK OVER THIS!
NOW, NOW, DEAR...
THUNK!

THAT'S THE MAIL! I'LL GET IT!
DING DONG

COUPLE OF ADS AND THE NEW ISSUE OF "FILM PIX"!
I'LL TAKE THAT!

BETTY! YOU HAVEN'T EVEN LOOKED AT IT!
AND I DON'T INTEND TO! I'M NOT TAKING ANY CHANCES!
THUNK!
END

FANTASTIC
FASHIONS
FOR
FABULOUS
FUN-TIMES

RONNIE IS CONSTANTLY REMINDING ME THAT WHENEVER I "SOLVE" A CRIME, IT'S ALWAYS BY DUMB LUCK! THIS TIME SHE COULD BE RIGHT!
Betty
in "GIVE ME A RING"
CHAPTER ONE
CRIME
AH-AHH-KYATCHEWWW!
059687123
13940192

(SNIFF!)... SURE GLAD I DON'T HAVE TO BE OUTSIDE WITH THIS NASTY HEAD COLD! (SNIFF!)... IT MUST BE FREEZING OUT THERE!

BING Z BONG Z
IF THAT'S THE PAPER BOY, I'LL BET HE COULD USE A CUP OF HOT CHOCOLATE!

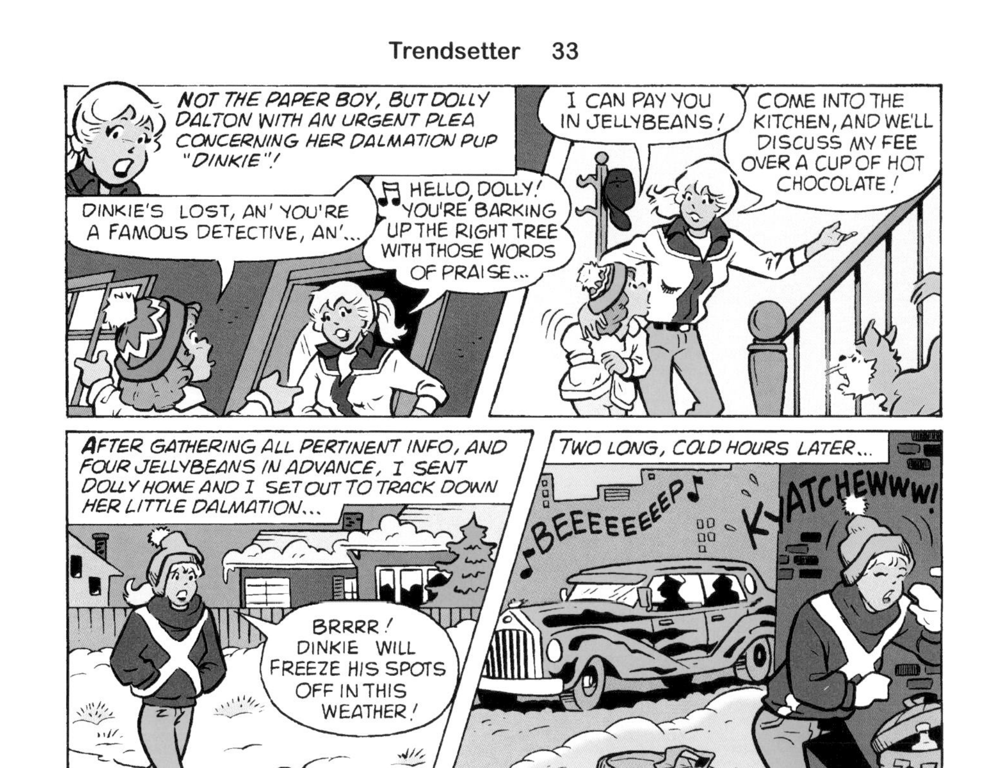
NOT THE PAPER BOY, BUT DOLLY DALTON WITH AN URGENT PLEA CONCERNING HER DALMATION PUP "DINKIE"!
DINKIE'S LOST, AN' YOU'RE A FAMOUS DETECTIVE, AN'...
HELLO, DOLLY! YOU'RE BARKING UP THE RIGHT TREE WITH THOSE WORDS OF PRAISE...
I CAN PAY YOU IN JELLYBEANS!
COME INTO THE KITCHEN, AND WE'LL DISCUSS MY FEE OVER A CUP OF HOT CHOCOLATE!
AFTER GATHERING ALL PERTINENT INFO, AND FOUR JELLYBEANS IN ADVANCE, I SENT DOLLY HOME AND I SET OUT TO TRACK DOWN HER LITTLE DALMATION...
BRRRR! DINKIE WILL FREEZE HIS SPOTS OFF IN THIS WEATHER!
TWO LONG, COLD HOURS LATER...
BEEEEEEEEEP
KYATCHEWWW!

HI, RON!
KYATCHEWW!
I HAVE A COLD! (SNIFF)
I CAN SENSE THAT! I'M VERY PERCEPTIVE! A CUP OF HERB TEA AND COLD MEDICINE WILL FIX SNEEZIES! JUMP IN, BUT DON'T SIT TOO CLOSE TO ME...

...RON HAS HER WARM SIDE...
KYATCHEWWW!
ON SECOND THOUGHT, BETTY, SIT UP FRONT!
I HADN'T FORGOTTEN DOLLY DALTON'S DALMATION DINKIE BUT THE THOUGHT OF HOT TEA WAS INVITING...
2

SMITHERS BROUGHT US HERBAL TEA AND SOME COLD MEDICINE, WHICH GUARANTEED ME NO MORE SNIFFS AND SNEEZES FOR EIGHT HOURS...
WHAT'S WITH ALL THE CRATES?
LODGE
LODGE

THOSE CRATES JUST ARRIVED FOR DADDY! THEY CONTAIN ANCIENT RELICS FROM TANGAPOON!
TANGAPOON, YOU SAY!?

TANGAPOON IS A TINY KINGDOM HIGH IN THE MOUNTAINS OF ANOTHER TIME ZONE! THEY DON'T DO MUCH THERE EXCEPT EXPORT A LOT OF YAK BUTTER!
HMMMM... THIS RING...
IT'S A MYSTIC RING! THE PRIZE OF DADDY'S COLLECTION... SUPPOSEDLY IT HAS SUPERNATURAL POWERS!
MYSTIC, SUPERNATURAL, YOU SAY?
UTTER THE SECRET WORD AND THE SPIRIT THAT LIVES IN THE RING WILL GRANT YOU ANY THREE WISHES! ONE CATCH, THO! NOBODY KNOWS THE SECRET WORD! IT'S ALL RUBBISH, IF YOU ASK ME!
THE RING IS STUCK ON MY FINGER...!
3

DADDY! YOUR TANGAPOONIAN RING...
... IT'S STUCK ON BETTY'S FINGER!
OUCH!
WHAT?!!

OUCH!!
EGAD! IT'S STUCK, ALL RIGHT!
GETTING IT OFF MAY TAKE TIME...

ER...I'VE GOT TO GO! I'M LOOKING FOR A LOST PUP! DOLLY DALTON'S DALMATION DINKIE!
THAT RING IS PRICELESS! I'VE JUST BEEN INFORMED THAT TANGAPOON AGENTS ARE HERE, TRACKING IT DOWN... WANTING TO RETURN IT TO THEIR KINGDOM!

I'M PHONING A PROTECTION AGENCY TO HAVE TWO BODYGUARDS HERE, PRONTO! THEY'LL GO EVERYWHERE WITH YOU!
EVERYWHERE, YOU SAY?
MOST EVERYWHERE!

MS. VERONICA, YOUR SEAMSTRESS IS HERE TO FIT YOU FOR YOUR BEGGAR'S OUTFIT FOR THE CHARITY COSTUME BALL!
NEATO!
AHHHH! ONLY FROM ANCIENT TANGA-POON COULD THERE COME SUCH ARTISTRY!

...ONE THING ABOUT REALLY WEALTHY PEOPLE... THEY HAVE A HABIT OF FORGET-TING ABOUT THE REST OF US...
I WANDERED DOWN TO THE FOYER...
4

AH! MY TWO BODYGUARDS HAVE ARRIVED! THAT WAS FAST!

SHE WEARS THE RING!!
HI, THERE! I WANT TO GO TO 33 THISTLEBROOK LA–

EEE-YIPE!!

DIPLOMAT
ROAR!

ONE DOESN'T HAVE TO BE A KEEN SUPER SLEUTHER TO FIGURE OUT THAT THESE TWO ARE NOT MY BODYGUARDS...
OUCH!
THE RING IS STUCK ON HER FINGER!!

WE WILL HAVE TO STARVE HER, UNTIL THE RING FALLS OFF! BY THAT TIME, WE'LL BE IN TANGAPOON!
TANGAPOON YOU SAY?!!
5

AS WE PRESENT HER TO OUR KING AS HIS SLAVE, THE RING WILL SLIDE FROM HER SHRUNKEN DIGIT!
ALL TANGAPOON WILL REJOICE!

GO TO TANGAPOON?!! HAH!! FAT CHANCE! YOU WON'T MAKE IT OUT OF TOWN! MR. LODGE WILL HAVE ALL THE ROADS, AIRPORTS AND BUS LINES COVERED! BETTER GIVE YOURSELVES UP!

HOOOOT!
ORIENT LINES

ROLL IT RIGHT INTO OUR CABIN, STEWARD!

COMFY, MY DEAR?
MMMFF!

I PROMISED TO BE QUIET IF THEY UNGAGGED ME, BUT I COULDN'T HELP DROOLING AS THEY CONSUMED THEIR FIRST MEAL!
THE CHICKEN DIVAN WAS DIVINE!
CARE FOR SOME MORE WATER, MY PET? I'VE SWEETENED IT WITH YAK BUTTER!
YECH TO YOU AND YOUR YAK BUTTER!
END CHAPTER ONE-
6

"GIVE ME A RING"
CHAPTER 2

I WAS FEELING MISERABLE! I WAS HUNGRY...
THE YAK BUTTER AND WATER TASTED TERRIBLE, AND THE COLD MEDICINE HAD WORN OFF! MY COLD WAS BACK WITH A VENGEANCE!
... MY ABDUCTORS RE-GAGGED ME AND WENT FOR A STROLL ON THE PROMENADE DECK...

I WAS BEGINNING TO LOSE HOPE, WHEN...
MY MAGNIFYING GLASS! MUST'VE FALLEN OUT OF MY POCKET AS I WAS TUMBLED AROUND!

WITH NO LITTLE DIFFICULTY, I PICKED IT UP ... AND PRAYED FOR OUR WINTER SUN TO KEEP ON SHINING...
PURE

...AFTER WHAT SEEMED AN ETERNITY...
SIZZZZLE...
SNAP!

WHEN YOU'RE REALLY STARVING, EVEN YAK BUTTER LOOKS GOOD...
PURE YAK BUTTER
I GRABBED IT...

URRK!
7

WEAK FROM LACK OF NOURISHMENT, MY BOUNDLESS TEENAGE ENERGY WAS ON THE WANE...
JUST ANOTHER REASON TO NEVER BE WITHOUT A CUP OF YAK BUTTER!
ENGINE ROOM AUTHORIZED PERSONNEL ONLY
?
RRR
DRRRRRRR
KLUNK!
8

DRRRRRNNNN
HALP! HALP!
OHH... THEY CAN'T HEAR ME!
KLUNK
WHIRRRRR

WHOOP
WHOOP!
WHOOOP!
PUFF! PUFF! PANT!
CHUGGA
CHUGGA
CHUGGA
TAPPA TAPPA TAPP
DRNNNNNNNNN
OUT TO LIFEBOATS
I'LL HIDE IN A LIFEBOAT! THEY DO THAT IN ALL THE SEA ADVENTURE YARNS! (SNIFF)
LOCKED!
TO LIFEBOAT
ENOUGH OF THIS! WE SHALL TAKE ONLY HER FINGER BACK TO TANGAPOON!
IT'S COMING WITH US NO MATTER HOW YOU SLICE IT!
YOU... YOU WOULDN'T! AH... AH...
KYATCHEWWWW!
ZOINK!
9

YII! THE MAGIC WORD! SHE STUMBLED UPON IT!
AND THAT'S NOTHING TO SNEEZE AT!
THE WEARER SHALL HAVE THREE WISHES... AND PERHAPS DISCOVER WHAT BLISS IS...
GET RID OF THESE TWO CREEPS!
IT SHALL BE DONE ...AND I WON'T USE A GUN!
POP!
WH-WHERE'D THEY GO?!
BACK TO TANGAPOON, VIA ASTRAL EXPRESS ...THEY'LL ARRIVE IN A TERRIBLE MESS!
OUT TO LIFEB
WHAT ELSE FOR YOU, PRETTY GIRL? C'MON! GIVE ME A WHIRL...
(SNIFF) I WANNA GO HOME!
POP!
YOU DID IT! I'M BACK IN MY ROOM!
THAT WASN'T EASY ...THESE FAST TRIPS MAKE ME QUEASY...
YOU HAVE BUT ONE WISH REMAINING ...THERE'S NO SENSE COMPLAINING...
...ONE WISH! WHY, I COULD BE AS WEALTHY AS RONNIE LODGE... EVEN WEALTHIER!!
WAIT! I KNOW!!
10

HELP ME LOCATE A LOST PUP... DOLLY DALTON'S DALMATION DINKIE!
DINKIE'S IN A FACTORY... NOW SHUT DOWN! IT'S ON THE SOUTH SIDE OF TOWN...

...THE ABANDONED PICKLE PACKING PLANT!
BETTER GET THERE SOONER THAN LATER ...DINKIE'S FREEZING IN THE SHAFT OF THE ELEVATOR!

THE MYSTIC RING WAS RIGHT ON! WITH ARCHIE'S HELP, WE RECOVERED DOLLY DALTON'S DALMATION DINKIE!

TO THIS DAY ARCHIE KNOWS NOTHING OF THE RING... I KEPT MY GLOVES ON AND MY CUPID'S BOW LIPS SEALED!

LATER:
I DON'T KNOW HOW TO THANK YOU! IS THERE ANYTHING I CAN DO FOR YOU?
I WANT TO RETURN HOME REAL SOON ...OH, CARRY ME BACK TO OL' TANGAPOON...

I WAS ABLE TO CONVINCE MR. LODGE THAT IN THE BEST INTERESTS OF OUR TWO COUNTRIES, THE RING SHOULD GO BACK TO TANGAPOON... THUS ASSURING AN UNINTERRUPTED FLOW OF YAK BUTTER TO THIS HEMISPHERE...
CARE FOR A JELLYBEAN?
THIS CASE IS CLOSED!
END

OH, HOW'D I REMOVE THE RING? EASY! I DIPPED MY RING FINGER INTO A JAR OF MR. LODGE'S IMPORTED YAK BUTTER...IT SLID RIGHT OFF!

Betty IN "PLASTER PARTING" (OR "IT WAS A CASTOFF BUT SHE KEPT IT!")
COOPER

DEAR DIARY, TONIGHT I WENT SKATING FOR THE FIRST TIME IN WEEKS!
RIVERDA
MY Diary
...IT WAS SURE INDUSTRIAL-STRENGTH HEAVEN... GLIDING ALONG WITH ARCHIE UNDER A FULL MOON...

...BUT A BROKEN LEG CAN BE QUITE AN EXPERIENCE! ... OR SHOULD I SAY "HASSLE?!"
I MEAN, A SIMPLE THING LIKE TAKING A SHOWER...
1

...WHILE BALANCING ON MY GOOD LEG WITH MY BROKEN ONE INSIDE A LAWN BAG TO KEEP THE CAST DRY...

AND THANK GOODNESS, NO MORE WHEELCHAIRS!
YEAH, BETS... MOOSE FOUND OUT I DATED MIDGE LAST NIGHT! GULP

DAD RENTED A WHEELCHAIR FROM GRANNY GROAN'S SICKROOM SUPPLIES ...LOCATED ON THE ROAD TO RUIN!
GRANNY GROAN'S
SICKROOM SUPPLIES

HA HA! I JUST MADE UP THE ADDRESS!

FINALLY, AFTER SIX WEEKS, CAME THE CAST CUTTING...
...CAREFUL, DOCTOR...
DOES THIS HURT, BETTY?
Bzzzzzz

NO! I WANT TO SAVE THIS CAST AND YOU'RE ABOUT TO SAW RIGHT THROUGH ARCHIE'S NAME!
MOOSE
Archie
DILTON

...MY LEG MUSCLES WERE WEAK, BUT I RAPIDLY GRADUATED FROM A CRUTCH TO A CANE!
POP'S
BUT I KINDA LIKED THAT PART BECAUSE...
2

...I COULD ALWAYS FIND ARCHIE TO LEAN ON!
JUST A COUPLE OF MORE STEPS, BETS!
OH, THANK YOU, ARCHIE!
...WHAT A PERFORMANCE!
BRAVO! BETTY DEAR, ARE YOU TAKING A DRAMA CLASS THIS YEAR?
CLAP! CLAP!
GIGGLE! IT REALLY VEXED VERONICA!
...BUT SOON, THE DRAWBACKS OF A HEALED LEG BECAME ALL TOO APPARENT...
My Diary
THIS ROOM HAS BEEN A MESS FOR WEEKS! NOW YOU CAN PICK IT UP!
BUT, MOM, I WON'T BE ABLE TO FIND ANYTHING!

...AND THE ERRANDS...!
BLESS OUR HOME
AND PUT SOME GAS IN THE CAR BEFORE YOU PICK UP DADDY AT THE OFFICE! THEN DROP THESE OFF AT THE DRY CLEANER ON THE WAY BACK...

I SHOVEL OUT THE DRIVEWAY...
3

...AND MY DANCING'S A LITTLE RUSTY...
...I'LL HAVE TO GIVE THAT SOME ATTENTION!

...AND I'M GIVING ATTENTION TO OTHER AREAS I DIDN'T ALWAYS THINK ABOUT...
TODAY'S SPECIAL
'TIL NOW...

...OH, I FORGOT ONE THING! AS YET, WE HAVEN'T TAKEN THE WHEELCHAIR BACK TO GRANNY GROAN'S SICKROOM SUPPLIES!

...I LOANED IT OUT... REAL FAST... RIGHT IN FRONT OF MY HOUSE, WHERE...

MOOSE FINALLY CAUGHT UP WITH REGGIE!!
TWEET
TWEET
COOPER
END

Betty and Veronica in The Grass is Always Greener
SO THIS IS WHERE WE'LL BE SPENDING OUR WINTER VACATION!
...IT'S QUITE IMPRESSIVE!
BETTY! WHAT ARE YOU DOING HERE?

I WAS LUCKY TO GET TAKEN ON BY THIS HOTEL DURING OUR SCHOOL BREAK!

I WAS LUCKY, TOO!
DADDY HIRED THE FAMOUS PIERRE LE MOGUL TO BE MY COACH WHILE WE'RE HERE!

WHAT A MAGNIFICENT BUFFET YOU SERVE HERE, BETTY!
I'VE NEVER SEEN ANYTHING LIKE IT!

I WISH YOU COULD JOIN US!
ACTUALLY, THE FOOD IN THE EMPLOYEE CAFETERIA ISN'T BAD AT ALL!

NO, NO, MISS VERONICA!!
UH, WHAT'S WRONG, PIERRE?!

I HAVE ZE SPECIAL HEALTH FOOD WAITING FOR YOU AT ZE TABLE!
HEALTH FOOD?

PIERRE IS A RENOWNED EXPERT ON PROPER DIET FOR ATHLETES!
IF YUCKY FOOD IS GOOD FOR SKIING, THEN I'M GUARANTEED GOLD AT THE NEXT OLYMPICS!

BETTY AT LEAST GETS TO EAT WHAT SHE LIKES!
EMPLOYEE CAFETERIA
2

I HEAR THE HOTEL HAS GREAT DISCO MUSIC!
SO LET'S GO DANCING TONIGHT, BETTY!
HOTEL HIVER
ENTERTAINMENT NIGHTLY

... SORRY, BUT THE HOTEL STAFF ISN'T ALLOWED TO MINGLE WITH THE GUESTS!
BUT WE GET TO DANCE IN OUR OWN DORM!

TOO BAD BETTY CAN'T ENJOY THE LIVE MUSIC!
-AND LOOK AT ALL THE HANDSOME DUDES!

WOW! THIS IS THE LIFE!

MISS VERONICA, IT IZ MUCH TOO LATE FOR YOU TO BE UP!
?

WE MUST GET UP AT FIVE TOMORROW!
...ZAT IZ WHEN ZE POWDER SNOW IZ AT ITS BEST!
DID YOU SAY FIVE?!
3

BESIDES, DISCO DANCING DEVELOPS ZE WRONG MUSCLES FOR SKIING!
FIVE? MAYBE HE MEANS 5 P.M.!
DISCO TONIGH

BETTY SEEMS TO BE HAVING FUN... EVEN IF IT'S JUST DANCING TO RECORDS!
10:05

AT ZE DAWN EVERYTHING IZ SO PEACEFUL AND QUIET!
BRRR! EXCEPT FOR MY CHATTERING TEETH!

AT LEAST THERE'S ONE CONSOLATION...
AT THIS HOUR WE DON'T HAVE TO GET ON ANY LONG LINE!
SKI LIFT

HA! ZE SKI LIFT IZ FOR SISSIES!
SKI LIFT

TO DEVELOP ZE STRONG LEG MUSCLES ONE MUST ATTACK ZE MOUNTAINS ON FOOT!
RIGHT NOW I'D RATHER BE ATTACKING MY BED!
4

HOW MANY MORE TIMES MUST WE SKI DOWN THIS HILL, PIERRE?
ZIS IZ ZE LAST TIME FOR TODAY, VERONICA!

... ZE REST OF ZE AFTERNOON, WE MUST RELAX!
THANK GOODNESS FOR THAT!

WE JUST RELAX WITH SOME NICE CROSS COUNTRY SKIING!

YAWN!
HI, BETTY! AREN'T YOU WORKING TODAY?
EMPLOYEE DORM

NO, IT'S MY DAY OFF!
HOW NICE!
I WISH I HAD A DAY OFF!

VERONICA IS SO FORTUNATE! SHE SKIS EVERY DAY!
OH, WELL! I'M HAPPY I CAN GET TO SKI AT ALL!
5

I SEE YOU'RE LEAVING TODAY TOO, RONNIE!
YES, ALL GOOD THINGS MUST COME TO AN END... INCLUDING VACATIONS!
CHECKOUT TIME: NOO

I THINK I HAD ALMOST AS MUCH FUN AS YOU THESE TWO WEEKS!
IT SEEMED MORE LIKE TWO YEARS!

GEE! SHE'S EVEN LEAVING IN A CHAUFFEURED LIMO!

YOU CAN RIDE WITH US... IF YOU DON'T MIND BEING A LITTLE CROWDED!
THANKS, BUT A CHARTERED BUS IS TAKING ME AND THE GANG HOME!

SHE'S GETTING TO GO HOME WITH ALL HER FRIENDS!

GOSH! HOW I ENVY VERONICA!
GOSH! HOW I ENVY BETTY!
CHARTER
The END

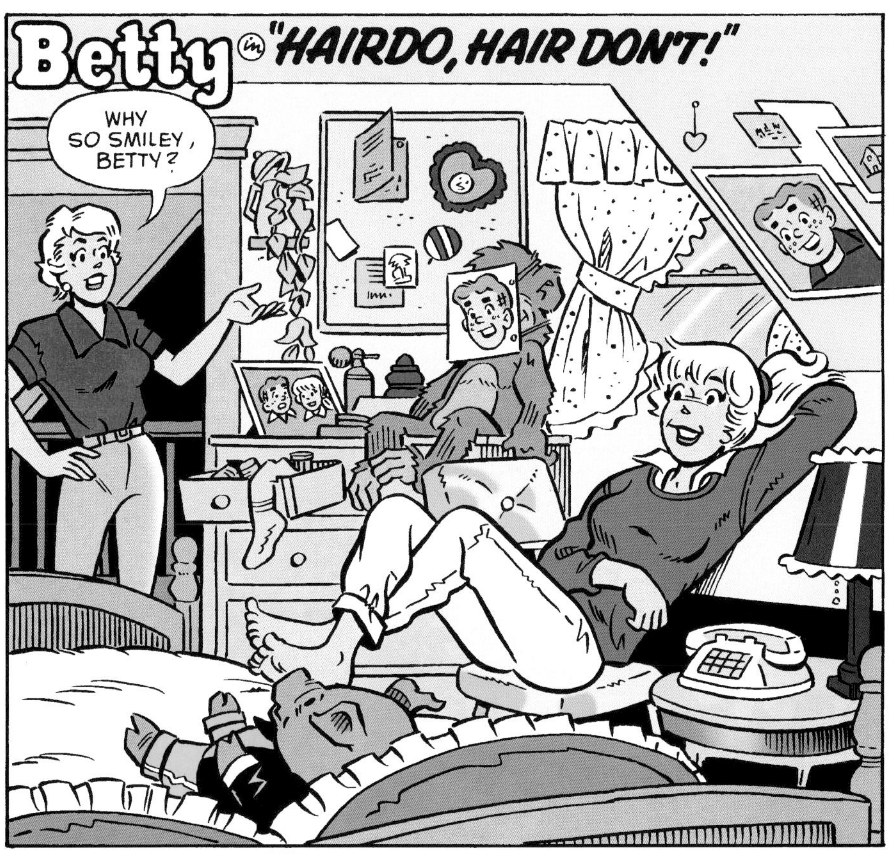
Betty in "HAIRDO, HAIR DON'T!"
WHY SO SMILEY, BETTY?

ARCHIE JUST CALLED TO INVITE ME ON A SPECIAL DATE TOMORROW!

HE'S TAKING ME TO A REALLY FANCY RESTAURANT!
OH, HOW NICE!

THAT'S A REAL CHANGE FROM BURGERS AT POP TATE'S!
HMMM... SPEAKING OF CHANGE...

...MAYBE I SHOULD CHANGE MY HAIR-STYLE INTO SOMETHING FANCIER FOR TOMORROW!

WHAT DO YOU THINK, MOM?
I THINK YOU LOOK FINE... BUT IT'S YOUR HAIR...

I THINK I'LL EXPERIMENT A BIT...
I HAVE TO GO OUT! I'LL SEE YOU LATER!

HOW ABOUT SOMETHING WITH MY HAIR UP...
PHHT!

(GULP!) NO WAY! I DON'T LIKE THE WAY MY EARS LOOK!
2

I'LL TRY SOME-THING ELSE...!
PHH FT!
I WANT JUST THE RIGHT STYLE!
BETTY TRIES SEVERAL NEW LOOKS...
PHFFT!
Lady Lovely
Hair Spray
DEFINITELY NOT!
UH-UH!
EEE-YUKK!!
NO WAY!
3

THIS TURNED OUT TO BE A DUMB IDEA! I'LL STICK WITH MY OLD STYLE! ... BUT NOW MY HAIR IS ALL STICKY!

I'D BETTER WASH IT SO IT'S NICE FOR TOMORROW!

OH, GEE! I'M OUT OF MY FAVORITE SHADE OF LIPSTICK! ...AND HAIRSPRAY, TOO!
RATTLE RATTLE
HAIR SPRAY

I'D BETTER GO TO THE STORE NOW! I MAY NOT HAVE TIME TOMORROW...

BRRRR! IT'S REALLY CHILLY OUT HERE!
WHOOSH!
4

THE NEXT DAY...
I'VE GOT IT!
RINNNNG!

AH-- CHOO.!! HI, ARCHIE, IT'S BEDDY!
HI, BETTY! ...YOU SOUND AWFUL!

AH-AH-CHOO!! ...I FEEL AWFUL TOO! I'M SORRY, BUT I'M TOO SICK TO GO OUT TONIGHT!

GOSH, I'M SORRY TOO! ...WHAT HAPPENED?

I WENT OUTSIDE RIGHT AFTER WASHING MY HAIR, AND I CAUGHT A TERRIBLE CODE!
END

Betty and Veronica
in
"HEAVENLY HELPER"
OH, RON! LOOK AT THAT POOR BOY! I THINK HE'S CLOSE TO TEARS!
HE IS A SAD-LOOKING LITTLE GUY! LET'S SEE IF WE CAN CHEER HIM UP SOMEHOW!

WHAT'S YOUR PROBLEM, LITTLE MAN? SOMEBODY STOLE YOUR LUNCH, RIGHT?
N-NO, MA'AM!
HEY! I KNOW! IT'S VERY COLD AND HE'S GOT NO HAT! I'LL BET HIS EARS ARE FROZEN!
HERE, SONNY! TRY THIS ON!

IT'S A BIT LARGE, BUT IT'LL KEEP THOSE EARS WARM!
GEE, THANKS, LADIES!
PLONK!

...AND HERE'S FIVE DOLLARS! GO GET YOURSELF A FEW HOT CHOCOLATES! THEY'LL FIX YOU UP!
WOW! YOU TWO ARE GOOD PEOPLE!

I SAW THAT! MAN! WHAT A COUPLE OF PATSIES!
WHATEVER DO YOU MEAN, REGGIE?

THAT PINT-SIZED CON MAN WILL PROBABLY SELL THAT EXPENSIVE FUR HAT AND ADD TO THE FIVE BUCKS HE GLOMMED FROM YOU!
HMPH! YOU'RE SUCH A CYNIC!

I'LL PROVE IT! I'M GONNA FOLLOW THE LITTLE TWERP! I'LL REPORT BACK LATER!
WE'LL AWAIT YOUR APOLOGY!

WITH SILENT STEALTH, THE GREAT PRIVATE EYE RELENTLESSLY PURSUES THE LARCENOUS LAD!
2

SNAKE, WILL YOU LOOK AT WHUT FATE HAS BRUNG US?
-AN' I WUZ JUST GONNA SAY IT WUZ A DULL DAY!
?

EEYIPE!!
T-THOSE KILLERS APPEARED LIKE MAGIC!

L-LET'S HOPE THEY'RE TOO MUSCLE-BOUND TO CLEAR THIS FENCE!
SCRABBLE
SCRATCH
SCRABBLE

ACK!
WHERE DID HE COME FROM? THESE PEOPLE DON'T HAVE A DOG!!
ARF!
GROWL!
SNARE!

EEP! HE'S GONE!! I MUST HAVE IMAGINED HIM!

MANTLE, YOU'RE CRACKIN' UP! SENILITY CAN'T SHOW UP AT SEVENTEEN, CAN IT?
3

HEY, MISTER! YOU STOPPED FOLLOWING ME! HOW COME?

AARGH!
YOU LITTLE MONSTER! GET OUTTA MY FACE

REGGIE! WHAT ARE YOU UP TO NOW?
IT'S THAT WEIRD KID! WAIT'LL I GET MY HANDS ON HIM!

WHAT'S WRONG WITH YOU, REGGIE? HE'S A FINE LITTLE BOY!
A LITTLE COMPASSION MIGHT SOFTEN YOUR HARD HEART!

EEP! RON! LOOK AT THIS! LYING RIGHT HERE ON THE GROUND!
WHAT IS IT?

ACK! TWO FRONT ROW TICKETS TO THE ROCK CONCERT AT THE STADIUM!
EEP!! THOSE THINGS ARE PRICE-LESS!
4

IT'S NOT FAIR! I'M MORE DESERVING THAN YOU TWO BLEEDING HEART DO-GOODERS!
WOW!!

SPLOOSH!
W-WHAT WAS THAT?

ACK! HE'S COVERED WITH MUD! WE HAVEN'T HAD RAIN IN A MONTH!
IT'S A MIRACLE OF SOME SORT!!

...AND LOOK!! HERE'S YOUR HAT AND FIVE DOLLAR BILL!
W-WHAT I GAVE THAT LITTLE BOY!

R-RON! D-DO YOU BELIEVE IN ANGELS?
IF YOU HAD ASKED ME YESTERDAY, I MIGHT HAVE SAID NO!!--- BUT...
SOMEBODY UP THERE HATES ME!
PLOP
PLIP
PLOP
PLOP
DRIP
END

Veronica in "STAR★STRUCK"

DAUGHTERS OF AMERICAN
MILLIONAIRES CLUB
ANNUAL WINTER SOIRÉE
WHAT A DULL PLACE! TOO BAD DADDY THINKS THE "DAUGHTERS OF AMERICAN BILLIONAIRES" CLUB IS FOR SNOBS!
VERONICA!!

LOOK AT THIS ITEM IN "SOAP STAR SPY" MAGAZINE! IT'S ABOUT BRETT BOLDER, THE GORGEOUS HUNK WHO PLAYS DR. BRAKEHART ON "THE YOUNG AND THE PAINLESS"!
WHAT ABOUT HIM?
SOAP STAR SPY

IT SAYS THAT HE'S GOING TO BE VISITING RELATIVES IN THE TOWN OF RIVERDALE!
RIVERDALE?!

YES! ISN'T THAT THE QUAINT LITTLE HAMLET WHERE YOU LIVE? I DON'T SUPPOSE YOU KNOW BRETT BOLDER!
HA! I DOUBT IT!

BRETT BOLDER IS, LIKE, THE MOST PRIVATE SOAP STAR! HE'S, LIKE, SO ALOOF AND HE NEVER MIXES WITH NOBODIES... LIKE VERONICA!
IS THAT SO!!

FOR YOUR INFORMATION, BRETT IS AN OLD AND DEAR FRIEND! WHY HE... HE'S PRACTICALLY FAMILY!

NOT THAT WE DOUBT YOU, RONNIE DEAR, BUT HOW ABOUT PRODUCING A PHOTO OF YOU AND BRETT TO SUPPORT YOUR... UH... FAIRY TALE!
YOU WANT A PHOTO? YOU'VE GOT IT!

SOON...
I KNOW I SHOULDN'T HAVE LIED, BUT THOSE RICH WITCHES REALLY TICK ME OFF! LUCKY FOR ME...

...I SUBSCRIBE TO 'SUPER SECRET SOAP STAR SPY' MAGAZINE! IT TELLS EVERYTHING ABOUT BRETT BOLDER, SO GETTING A PHOTO WITH HIM SHOULD BE NO PROBLEM!
SUPER SECRET SOAP STAR SPY MAGAZINE
2

THIS ARTICLE SAYS THAT HE LOVES HIS DOG, A WHEATEN TERRIER NAMED OPHIE! IT SAYS THAT BRETT WALKS IT AND CARES FOR IT PERSONALLY! HMMM...
SUPER SECRET
SOAP STA

... I THINK I'LL GET A DOG AND A PHOTOGRAPHER AND GO FOR A WALK IN RIVERDALE PARK! THERE'S NO TELLING WHO I'LL RUN INTO THERE!
RIVERDALE AIRPORT
ROUTE 17-A
NEXT EXIT 5 MI.

DAYS LATER...
THERE HE IS! HE'S EVEN MORE GORGEOUS IN PERSON! AS SOON AS I STRIKE UP A CONVERSATION WITH HIM, SNAP OUR PICTURE!
YES, MS. LODGE!

HEY! WAIT FOR ME!
ERF!

ERF! ERF!
ROWF!
OH, NO! OPHIE IS AFRAID OF SMALL...
3

... DOGS!!
EEEYAAHHH!
ERF! ERF! ERF!

THAT DIDN'T WORK OUT SO WELL! I'LL GET A LARGER DOG AND TRY AGAIN!

NEXT DAY...
BRETT IS HAVING HIS DOG GROOMED HERE! I CALLED AND TOOK THE APPOINTMENT RIGHT AFTER HIM! YOU CAN PHOTOGRAPH US THROUGH THE FRONT WINDOW!
GOTCHA!
The PAMPERED PET

HI! WE'RE A BIT EARLY! I HOPE YOU DON'T MIND IF I STARE...ER... I MEAN WATCH!
NOT AT ALL, MS. LODGE!

OPHIE! NO!
ROWF!
4

KER-SPLASH!

(BLUB) OPHIE DOESN'T GET ALONG WITH POODLES! COULD YOU LEAVE TILL WE'RE DONE?!
OF COURSE! (GULP!) DOWN, OPHIE!
ARF!
ROWF!

LATER THAT WEEK...
RIVERDALE DOG SHOW
THIS DOG SHOW IS MY LAST CHANCE TO GET A PHOTO WITH BRETT BEFORE HE LEAVES TOWN! BUT IN ORDER TO SHOW MY DOG IN THE SAME GROUP...

... I HAD TO BUY AN EXPENSIVE WHEATEN TERRIER, JUST LIKE THE TEMPERAMENTAL MUTT THAT BRETT OWNS!

HMPH! HE'S WEARING SHADES AND A HAT SO THAT FANS WON'T RECOGNIZE HIM!
MAYBE HE'S TRYING TO HIDE FROM YOU!
5

LADIES AND GENTLEMEN! OUR NEXT GROUP IS THE TERRIERS!
THAT'S US! LET'S GO, POOCH!

OUR DOGS SEEM TO LIKE EACH OTHER!
THAT'S A BEAUTIFUL TERRIER YOU'VE GOT THERE!
WOOF!
WOOF!

SIGH! DO YOU REALLY THINK SO?
HI, GIRL... HEY!!
SLURP

LOOK! IT'S BRETT BOLDER!!
EEEEEK!
OH, NO!
I'VE GOT TO GET OUT OF HERE!
6

BRETT! BRETT! I LOVE YOU!!
I'M SURROUNDED!

BRETT!!
HELP!
BRETT!! BRETT!!

THE FOLLOWING WEEK...
VICKI? THIS IS AMBER! I JUST GOT AN ENVELOPE IN THE MAIL FROM VERONICA LODGE AND GUESS WHAT... SHE DOES KNOW BRETT BOLDER!

UH-HUH... THAT'S RIGHT! AND SHE SENT ME A PHOTO TO PROVE IT! YES... BUT THERE'S ONE THING THAT PUZZLES ME, VICKI...

IT'S A VERY STRANGE PHOTO!
END

Betty and Veronica in CENTS OF VALUE
UH, OH! CAREFUL, BETTY! WE'RE ABOUT TO BECOME TARGETS OF THREE TERRIBLE TOTS!
HMPH! THE LITTLE SCAMPS! THEY SHOULD KNOW BETTER THAN TO PICK ON A SUPERIOR FORCE!

DUCK! THEY'RE LETTING LOOSE THEIR BARRAGE!

HOLD IT! THEY WEREN'T WINGING AT US!
...OR ELSE THEY'RE BADLY IN NEED OF PRACTICE!

LOOK! THEY'RE BELTING THAT POOR LITTLE GUY!!
WELL, AT LEAST THEY WERE SPORT ENOUGH TO PICK ON AN INFERIOR TARGET!
WHAP!
SPLAT!

HEY! LAY OFF, YOU LITTLE MONSTERS!
C'MON, BETTY! KIDS WILL BE KIDS!

THEY'RE LITTLE BULLIES! IT'S NOT A FAIR FIGHT!!

AND IT'S NONE OF YOUR BUSINESS! LET THE LITTLE GUY FIGHT HIS OWN BATTLES!
NOT WHILE I'M HERE TO EVEN THE SCORE! STEP ASIDE!!

BEGONE, YOU BULLIES!!
YIPE!
ZOOM!
WHOOSH!
SPLAT
WHERE DID THAT COME FROM?
S-SOMEONE WITH A GREAT ARM!!
OUCH!!
2

LET'S GET OUTTA HERE!!
ACK! DOESN'T SHE EVER MISS?
SPLAT!

YOU SPOILED A GOOD FIGHT!
IT WASN'T FAIR! LOOK AT THE SIZE OF THIS LITTLE GUY!
BRUSH! BRUSH!

GEE, LADY! THANKS FOR SAVING MY LIFE!
THAT'S ALL RIGHT, SONNY!

NO! I GOTTA SHOW MY 'PRECIATION! HERE! I WANT YOU SHOULD HAVE MY LUCKY PENNY!
YOU DON'T HAVE TO DO THAT!

PLEASE! I WANT YOU TO HAVE IT!
HA! IT WASN'T BRINGING YOU MUCH LUCK A WHILE AGO, KID!

IT BROUGHT ME THIS NICE LADY TO CHASE THOSE BIG KIDS!
AND YOU THINK YOUR STUPID PENNY DID THAT? WHO ARE YOU KIDDING?
3

OKAY, GUYS! LET'S PUT THAT BIG BLONDE ENEMY OUT OF COMMISSION!
REVENGE IS SWEET!

ACK! THOSE LITTLE MONSTERS ARE BACK!
WHIZZ!
ZOOM!

?
SWERVE!
ZOOM!
ZOOM!
ZOOM!
ZOOM!
SWERVE!
SWERVE!

WHAM!
WHAP!
SPLAT!

D-DID YOU SEE THE CURVES ON THOSE SNOWBALLS? IT MUST BE THE LUCKY PENNY!!
THAT'S THE CRAZIEST THING I EVER HEARD!!

PENNIES ARE WORTHLESS! KNOW WHAT I DO WITH THEM? HERE! I'VE GOT FOUR OF THEM IN MY POCKET!
4

HEY! VERONICA!
HI, DILTON!

IT'S NOT LIKE YOU TO LOSE MONEY!
PENNIES AREN'T MONEY! KEEP THEM, DILTON!!

GREAT! HEY! THIS ONE IS A COLLECTOR'S ITEM! IT'S WORTH HUNDREDS OF DOLLARS!

GEE! THAT WAS A LUCKY PENNY YOU THREW AWAY!
BAH! TELL ME ABOUT IT! C'MON! I'LL BUY YOU A HOT CHOCOLATE!
POP'S

GOSH! I'M RUNNING OUT OF SMALL CHANGE! DO YOU MIND PENNIES, VERONICA?
I'LL TAKE ALL YOU'VE GOT! I LOVE PENNIES, POPS!
?
HAMBURGER
SUNDAE $1.25
POP'S
END

Betty and Veronica in "WEIGHT and SEE"
GETTING A BIT CHUBBY, AREN'T YOU, FRIEND? THAT'S A HALF-POUND HEAVIER THAN THE LAST TIME WE WEIGHED IN TOGETHER!
WELL, A HALF-POUND ISN'T ENOUGH TO PANIC OVER! YOUR TURN TO HIT THE SCALES, RON!

HAH! NOT TO WORRY! THIS PERFECT BODY NEVER VARIES A FRACTION!
YIPE!
I NEED A NEW SCALE! THIS STUPID THING SAYS I'VE GAINED A HALF-POUND TOO!
FORGET IT! LIKE I SAID, IT'S NO BIG DEAL!

OF COURSE IT'S A BIG DEAL!! IF THAT SCALE ISN'T BROKEN, I'M TURNING TO FLAB!
OH, COME ON, NOW!

DON'T MAKE LIGHT OF THIS, GIRL! WE'VE GOT TO WORK THIS FAT OFF! STARTING *NOW*!
"*WE*"?

AEROBICS, MASSAGE, SAUNA! THE WORKS! LET'S GO!!
W-ELL ... IT'S NOT A BAD IDEA, I GUESS!

WE'LL START FIRST THING IN THE MORNING!!
NO WAY!

NOW! RIGHT NOW!! THIS SORT OF THING CAN'T BE PUT OFF!
JUST *POSTPONED* UNTIL TOMORROW!

NOT A CHANCE! COME ON! INTO MY EXERCISE ROOM!
I PROMISED TO HAVE LUNCH WITH A FRIEND!
2

YOU CAN LUNCH WITH A FRIEND ANYTIME! THIS IS IMPORTANT!
SORRY! A PROMISE IS A PROMISE!

ALL RIGHT! GO AHEAD! BUT YOU'LL BE SORRY WHEN I OUTSLIM YOU BY *POUNDS*!

GOOD GRIEF! THAT GIRL CAN PANIC OVER ABSOLUTELY *NOTHING*!

RIGHT ON TIME, BETTY! WHAT'LL IT BE? BURGERS, FRIES AND SODA?
SOUNDS GOOD TO ME!

HONESTLY, ARCHIE! YOU SHOULD HAVE HEARD THE FUSS SHE MADE OVER A HALF-POUND!
SHOOT! RON HAS ALWAYS BEEN FAMOUS FOR MAKING MOUNTAINS OUT OF MOLEHILLS!

I'LL BET SHE'S SWEATING BULLETS RIGHT NOW, TRYING TO GET RID OF IT!
COUNT ON IT!
3

A-ONE AND A-TWO AND A-THREE AND A-FOUR! ONE MORE (GASP) TIME!

GET 'EM UP! (PANT) HIGHER! LIFT 'EM HIGHER!

IT'S NOT LIKE YOU TO WORK UP A SWEAT, DEAR! WHAT'S THE OCCASION?
PANT!
PANT!
PUFF!

I'M TURNING INTO FLAB CITY, DADDY! IT'S GOT TO COME OFF!

DON'T OVERDO IT, DEAR! LOSING WEIGHT CAN'T BE RUSHED!
WHEW! I'M BUSHED! MAYBE THE SAUNA WILL MELT IT OFF!

BETTY IS A FOOL TO NEGLECT THAT EXTRA POUNDAGE, EVEN FOR A MOMENT!
4

MAINTAINING THIS STATE OF PERFECTION IS A CONSTANT JOB!

WELL, I FINISHED MY LUNCHEON DATE, RON! SHALL WE START THOSE EXERCISES?
HAH! CHECK THIS OUT, CHUBBY! LET ME AT THAT SCALE!

THERE! I LOST THAT EXTRA HALF-POUND! LET'S SEE HOW MUCH YOU PUT ON AT LUNCH!
OKAY!

WELL, HOW DO YOU LIKE THAT? I DROPPED TWO POUNDS! I GUESS IT'S MY METABOLISM!
ARRGH!! Y-YOU LOST WEIGHT?

PUT ON ANOTHER BURGER, POP! AND ANOTHER ORDER OF FRIES! IF IT WORKS FOR HER, IT'LL WORK FOR ME!!
SHE EXPECTS TO LOSE WEIGHT BY EATING?
HEY! I NEVER GET FAT!
SAVE THE BURGER
END

SABRINA
in
"SWIFT GIFT"

DARN! I MISSED THE MAIL PICK-UP!
DELICATESSE
U.S. MAIL
USE ZIP CODE

I WISH THIS CHRISTMAS CARD GETS TO ARCHIE ON TIME!
AND I'LL GRANT BETTY'S WISH!

SPIRIT WORLD, SEE THAT ARCHIE GETS THE CHRISTMAS CARD IMMEDIATELY!
ZAP

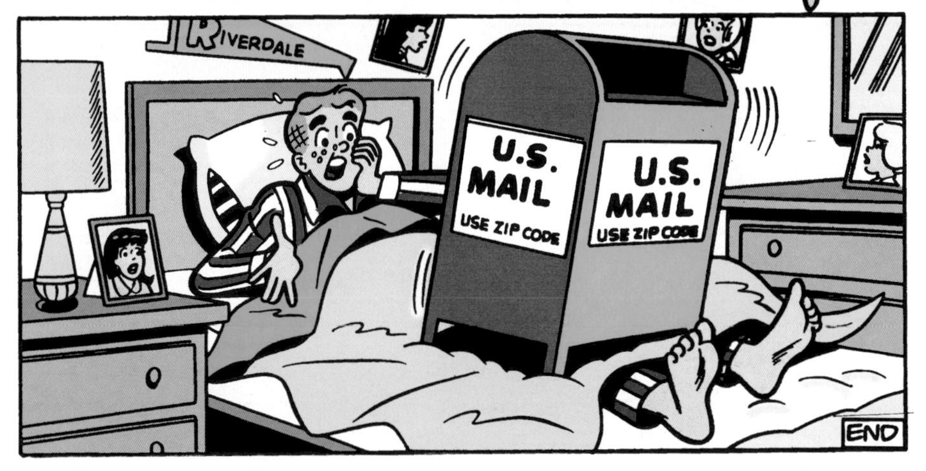
RIVERDALE
U.S. MAIL
USE ZIP CODE
U.S. MAIL
USE ZIP CODE
END